The Muppets Go Camping

STARRING JIM HENSON'S MUPPETS™

By Jocelyn Stevenson • Illustrated by Bruce McNally

Muppet Press/Random House

Library of Congress Cataloging in Publication Data: Stevenson, Jocelyn. The Muppets go camping. SUMMARY : Follows
the misadventures of the Muppets as they try to help Robin win his Frog-in-the-Wilds Badge for Frog Scouts.
[1. Camping—Fiction] I. McNally, Bruce. II. Title. PZ7.S8476Mu [E] 80-20261 AACR1 ISBN: 0-394-84711-3
Manufactured in the United States of America   5 6 7 8 9 0

"Ah, time to relax," sighed Kermit the Frog, as he settled down in his easy chair. "Hmmmm, what's this? Looks like a note from Robin."

Dear Uncle Kermit,
    I have gone to spend a night in the woods. I'm trying to win my Frog-in-the-Wilds Badge for Frog Scouts. I can't take any food. I must forage. But it's all right. I have one box of matches to make a fire.
    See you tomorrow.
        Love, Robin.

A little later,
Kermit was working
in his garden.
Lucky Robin, he
thought. Nothing like
a peaceful night
in the woods.

Just then, Fozzie Bear stopped by the gate. "Hi, Kermit!" he said. "What's new?"

"Robin's gone camping," said Kermit. He handed Robin's note to Fozzie.

"Kermit, this is terrible!" Fozzie said. "Poor Robin! He'll starve! He'll freeze! And there are scary things in the woods–like bears! You've got to protect him!"

"Okay," said Kermit.
"I wouldn't mind a peaceful
night in the woods.
I'll go camp near Robin.
If he needs help,
I'll be right there."
"Great idea," said Fozzie.
"I'll go too."

Suddenly Kermit had company.
"Count me in!" said Gonzo.
"And moi," said Miss Piggy.
"I'm with you, man,"
said Floyd Pepper.
"Camping! Camping!" bellowed Animal.
"There goes one peaceful night
in the woods," sighed Kermit.

Kermit told his friends to go home and pack.
"Don't forget to bring warm socks and sleeping bags," he said.
Fifteen minutes later, the rescue party set out to find Robin.
They'd brought warm socks and sleeping bags and a tuba
and shovels and an umbrella and costumes from the theater.
They trudged up a steep hill…

...into a dark and tangled forest.
"Wow! A swamp!" said Gonzo.
"It's fantastic! Let's camp here."
"No, I think we'd better keep going,"
said Kermit.

"Sleep in tree!" insisted Animal.

"Let's keep going," said Kermit.

"Man, I do like ditches," yawned Floyd. He lay down in a ditch and fell asleep.

"Well, er, I think we've walked far enough," said Kermit. "Let's set up camp in this clearing and have something to eat. Then we'll find Robin."

Sweetums put up the tent.
"Sweetums, is that the way a tent's
supposed to look…sir?" asked Fozzie.
"YES!!!" answered Sweetums.
"Looks terrific!" said Fozzie.

"Now for some food," said Kermit. He looked
in the food bag. "Er, I've got good news and bad news,"
he said. "The good news is we brought a nice, big
food bag. And the bad news is we forgot the food."

They all groaned.

"Well," said Miss Piggy, "if helpless little
Robin can camp without food, so can we. So why
doesn't somebody just run down to the store and
buy a nice, yummy dinner?"

"We can't *buy* food in the woods," said Kermit.
"We'll forage! We'll hunt! There's plenty to eat...
berries, fish, and don't forget dragonflies!
It's all out there waiting for us!"

"Ah-haaa!" said Fozzie.
"I'll be the berry hunter. Get it?
Bear-y hunter? Wocka, wocka!"

"And I'll be the fisherman,"
said Gonzo. "I'll be great!
I'll catch the biggest fish
you ever saw!"

"That's all you found?"
asked Kermit, when they came
back to camp.

"Yeah, but you should have
seen the one that got away!"
bragged Gonzo.

Sweetums made a fire,
while Floyd made dinner.

Kermit looked into the pot. "Shoe and Berry Stew," he gulped. "Nice going, gang."

After they ate some stew, Fozzie said, "We'd better start looking for Robin. He's probably starving."

"Good idea," said Kermit. "But remember, we're only here to help him if he needs help."

But finding Robin wasn't easy.

They found
his cap
and a match,
but no Robin.

"Here are some flipperprints,"
said Kermit. "Robin must be
around here somewhere."

They followed the flipperprints all the way
to a deep, dark cave.

"I knew it! I told you!" cried Fozzie.
"Poor Robin's been frognapped by bears!"

"Fozzie, there is no such thing as frognapping!"
said Kermit, waving his arms. "Now, let's see
if Robin is in the cave."

"You go first," said Fozzie, backing away.

Kermit was about to creep into the cave
when Floyd shouted, "Wait! More flipperprints!"
    They followed Robin's tracks to a deserted old house.
The roof had holes in it, and the shutters banged
in the howling wind.
    "I bet a witch lives here," whispered Gonzo.
    "A-a-a-anybody h-h-home?" called Kermit.
    No-one answered, except an owl: "Whooooooo!"
    They all ran away!

"I'm freezing," said Floyd.

"I'm starving," said Miss Piggy.

"I'm scared," said Fozzie.

"I'm Gonzo," said Gonzo.

"I think Robin's in trouble," said Fozzie.

"I *know we're* in trouble, man," said Floyd. "We're lost!"

"No, we're not," said Kermit. "Look, there's a light through the trees!"

"Light! Light!" shouted Animal, running toward the glow.

The others ran after him, tripping over the twisted roots in the path.

"Oof!" said Sweetums as he ran into Fozzie who ran into Miss Piggy who ran into Floyd who ran into Animal.

"Look at that!"
they shouted.
     They were back at
their camp. But it
sure wasn't the same!

The tent was sturdy, the fire was blazing,
and the hungry campers could smell fish and wild
mushrooms simmering in the pot.
"Who did this?" asked Kermit.

"I did," said a little green figure, stepping into the light of the campfire. It was Robin! "I found your camp and saw how much help you needed, so I..."

"ROBIN!" They all ran to greet the little frog.
"Were the bears nice to you?" asked Fozzie.
"And what about the witch?" asked Gonzo.
"Where have you been?" asked Kermit.
"All over the place, Uncle Kermit," said Robin.
"First, I set up camp, and then I foraged for food.
I caught a big fish and found lots of berries. After I ate,
I found a swell cave and a nifty little house. When it
got dark, I started back. Then I saw your tent and
knew you were in trouble. Was it the bears who
messed it up? And did a witch put a shoe in your stew?"

"Yes,...I mean, no,...um,
funny you should ask," said Kermit.
    Just then, Sweetums picked
Robin up and gave him a big,
sloppy kiss.

The next day, Robin won two awards.
His Frog Scout leader gave him the Frog-in-the-Wilds
Badge for camping alone in the woods and a
very special badge that said:
For Helping Campers in Trouble!